FOCUS ON THE FAMILY PRESENTS

Hunt for the Devil's Dragon

BOOK 11

MARIANNE HERING • WAYNE THOMAS BATSON
CREATIVE DIRECTION BY PAUL McCUSKER
ILLUSTRATED BY DAVID HOHN

TYNDALE

FOCUS ON THE FAMILY • ADVENTURES IN ODYSSEY
TYNDALE HOUSE PUBLISHERS, INC. • CAROL STREAM, ILLINOIS

Hunt for the Devil's Dragon
Copyright © 2013 Focus on the Family.

ISBN: 978-1-58997-738-9

A Focus on the Family book published by Tyndale House Publishers, Inc., Carol Stream, Illinois 60188

Focus on the Family and Adventures in Odyssey, and the accompanying logos and designs, are federally registered trademarks, and The Imagination Station is a federally registered trademark of Focus on the Family, Colorado Springs, CO 80995.

TYNDALE and Tyndale's quill logo are registered trademarks of Tyndale House Publishers, Inc.

Cover design by Michael Heath | Magnus Creative

Cataloging-in-Publication Data for this book is available by contacting the Library of Congress at www.loc.gov/help/contact-general.html.

Printed in the United States of America
2 3 4 5 6 7 8 9 / 17 16 15 14 13

For manufacturing information regarding this product, please call 1-800-323-9400.

For our source of hope, the Lord, Maker of Heaven and Earth: Use this tale to bring hope to those in need and courage to those who live in fright.

—WTB

Contents

A Root-Beer Float

"It's not fair," Beth muttered to herself. She was walking into Whit's End.

She walked past several customers. They sat at tables eating ice cream.

Whit was busy behind the counter. He smiled at her. "Hi, Beth. What can I get for you?" he asked.

"A double scoop of ice cream, please," Beth said, "with root beer."

She sat on a stool and folded her arms on

the counter. Then she
rested her chin on her arms.

Whit slid the foamy root-beer float
across the counter. "Do you want to tell me
what's wrong?" he asked kindly.

"Hey, Beth!" a familiar voice called from
behind her.

Beth turned around and
saw her cousin Patrick
walk into Whit's End.
He approached
the ice-cream
counter.
A large
backpack
was slung
over his

shoulder. He dropped it onto the stool next to Beth.

"You have a lot of books there," Whit said.

Patrick nodded. "Yep," he said. "I've got a science report to do."

"Let me know if you need help," Whit said.

"Uh-oh," Patrick said. "I see a two-scoop root-beer float. What's wrong, Beth?"

Whit looked to Beth for her answer.

"I had trouble at school," Beth said. "It was during recess."

"What happened?" Whit asked.

"Leslie Wazzek and her friends ganged up on Rachel," Beth said. "Leslie said that Rachel cheated off her during a math test."

"I know Rachel," Whit said. "I have a hard time believing she'd ever cheat."

"That's just it," Beth said. "Rachel didn't

cheat on the test."

"And if she was going to cheat," Patrick added, "she wouldn't cheat off *Leslie*! Leslie couldn't add two sticks together using all her fingers . . . *and* a calculator. She's about as smart as—"

"We've got the idea," Whit said to Patrick. He turned to Beth. "Why are you upset about an accusation that isn't true?"

"Because Leslie and her friends teased Rachel the entire recess. Finally Rachel started crying and ran inside," Beth said.

"You saw all of this?" Whit said.

Beth nodded. "I was right there," she said sadly. "I *should* have done something to stick up for Rachel. But I didn't. I was . . . afraid."

"Afraid of what?" Whit asked.

"Afraid of Leslie turning on me," Beth said. "She says mean things about people."

"Yeah, that's Leslie, all right," Patrick said.

Beth lowered her head. "I'm such a wimp," she said.

Whit gazed at her a moment. "We all have moments of feeling afraid," he said softly. "But that doesn't mean we're cowards."

"What do you mean?" Beth asked.

"The two of you should come with me," Whit said.

Beth looked up at him. "An adventure in the Imagination Station?" she asked.

Whit nodded. "Have you ever seen a dragon?" he asked.

"A dragon!" Patrick cried out.

Whit smiled and motioned for them to follow him.

● ● ●

Beth sat inside the Imagination Station. It was like the front end of a helicopter.

"Where are we going?" she asked. The idea of meeting a dragon made her feel curious. And a little uneasy.

"To England, right?" Patrick asked. "That's where all the dragons were. King Arthur killed one, I think."

Whit laughed. "No, not England," he said. "And you're not going to meet King Arthur. This adventure takes place in northern Africa. You're going to meet a man named Georgius."

"You really think this will help?" Beth asked. "With Leslie and Rachel, I mean."

Whit raised an eyebrow. "Are you all right, Beth?" he asked.

Beth shrugged. "I don't know which scares me more," she said. "Leslie Wazzek or meeting a dragon."

Whit chuckled. "There's only one way to find out. Are you ready?"

The cousins nodded.

Whit tapped a button, and the door slid closed. The red button on the dashboard began to blink. Beth pushed it. The machine began to shake. There was a loud hum. Then everything went black.

Hide-and-Seek

"When did you arrive?" a boy asked. His eyes were big, and his skin was dark. "My name is Hazi," he said. He gave her a curious look.

Beth felt startled. A second ago she had been sitting in the Imagination Station. Now she was standing before a boy named Hazi.

He was dressed in a tunic with colorful stripes. He pushed a round cloth hat to the side of his head. He blinked a lot.

Beth glanced at Patrick. He looked

confused too. He pointed to his clothes.
He was dressed in a tunic like Hazi's. But
Patrick had a thick coil of rope draped
around one shoulder.

Rope? Beth thought. *I wonder what kind
of adventure Mr. Whittaker has planned.*

Beth also wore a colorful tunic. Except
hers had a shiny green belt. On her feet
were sandals.

She put her hand inside her tunic
pocket. She found a metal nail file. She
looked at her short, clean nails. *Do I need a
manicure?* she wondered.

There were planks of wood under her feet.
And water sparkled in the gaps between
the wood. Around her were tall stacks
of beautiful folded cloths. There were fat
barrels, too. And decorated pots.

Beth heard shouting in the distance. It sounded like men at work.

A nearby voice startled Beth. "I'm Sabra," the voice said.

A tall girl stepped up next to the boy. Sabra looked a lot like Hazi. But her eyes were bigger. And her hair was longer. She wasn't wearing a hat.

Beth guessed they were brother and sister.

"Where are we?" Patrick asked.

"You're an odd one, my friend," Hazi said. "This is Leptis Magna. It's one of the greatest port cities in Libya."

Hazi motioned toward some piles of fabric. He said, "You're standing next to my father's imported goods. My father is a wealthy merchant, you see."

"Hazi!" Sabra said. "Don't be so boastful.

Besides, these two must be rich as well.
Look at the colorful fabric in their clothes."

"You must be right, my sister," Hazi said.
"Surely they came to Leptis on a boat like us."

"What are your names?" Sabra asked.

"I'm Beth," she said. "And this is my
cousin Patrick."

"Ah, fine names," Hazi said. He clapped
his hands. "Fine names for new friends.
Come and play with us."

"Yes, yes," Sabra said. "You must play. It
was such a long, boring boat ride."

Patrick and Beth looked at each other and
then shrugged. What else could they do?

They followed their new friends. Hazi
led them through a maze of crates. They
discovered they were on a long dock. Several
tall ships were anchored there.

Men and women in tunics or long robes wandered about. They looked as if they were shopping. Other people were dressed in rags. They carried heavy crates down from the ships.

But the shine of gold caught Beth's attention. Standing at every corner on every dock were soldiers. The men wore golden chest armor and long red capes. They carried spears and short swords.

Roman soldiers, Beth thought. She had seen them before on another Imagination Station adventure.

Hazi stopped at a stack of crates not far from the shoreline. He opened a crate and took out two brown pieces of cloth. "Let's play slaves-and-masters," he said. "You can pretend to be slaves. Sabra and I will be your masters."

Beth looked at the men in rags. "I'm not sure I like the sound of that game," Beth said. "Slavery isn't a game."

"What about hide-and-seek," Sabra said. "It's great fun."

Beth wondered what Mr. Whittaker would think. She knew he hadn't sent them back in history just to play games.

Patrick seemed to be thinking the same thing.

Before they could speak, Hazi said, "The rules are simple. We must stay on the dock. No getting onto a ship or hiding along the shore. And no dropping into the water. Sabra will seek us."

"Not fair, Hazi," Sabra said. "You always get to hide first."

"You see how mean she is?" Hazi asked.

"I'll seek first," Beth said. "I don't mind."

Sabra and Hazi scattered away from Beth.

Patrick hesitated and then rushed away.

Beth put her head down on a pile of cloth.
She closed her eyes. "One, two, three . . ."
She counted to twenty-one. Then she lifted
her head and looked around.

Beth made her way through the crowds
of people. No one seemed to notice her.
She went to stacks of boxes that had been
grouped in rows. She peeked around them.

A group of soldiers passed by. One of
them glared at her. She moved farther in
among the crates.

"Hazi! Sabra!" a deep voice shouted. The
voice was so loud that several people turned
to stare. Beth turned too.

The voice came from a short, stocky man. He wore a fine robe and colorful silk scarves.

"The wagon is loaded, my children," the stocky man called. "It's time we go home!"

Hazi popped up from inside a tall, round pot. "Aww," he said, "this was my best hiding place!"

The man waved at Hazi. "Bring your sister," he said. Then he walked toward the land end of the dock.

Suddenly, Sabra and Patrick were at Beth's side.

"Come with us and meet Father," Hazi said.

Hazi and Sabra hurried to shore. Many people were walking about. The cousins followed them through the crowd.

The stocky man was tying down the cargo on a covered wagon. "Ah, my children," the man said. He smiled broadly at Hazi and Sabra and gathered them in a hug.

"Father," Sabra said, "I'd like you to meet our new friends. This is Patrick. And Beth."

"Greetings to you!" the man said. "I'm Tarek of Silene!"

He had a thick, rounded beard that was black with flecks of gray.

Before Beth or Patrick could answer, a shadow fell over them.

A deep voice said, "What's this, Tarek? Two new workers who weren't on your scroll? It's unlike you to cheat Rome. You know there's a tax on all newcomers to Leptis Magna."

Beth looked up. She saw several Roman soldiers on horseback. The one who had been speaking wore a tall golden helmet.

"I've never cheated Rome," Tarek said. "And I've not begun today, Prefect Lucius."

"I see," Lucius said. His hair was almost as red as his cape. "Then how do you account for these two? They tried to hide from my soldiers on the docks."

"They were merely playing hide-and-seek," Tarek said. He turned to Patrick and Beth and gestured. "Tell the noble prefect that you aren't my workers."

"We're not his workers," Patrick said simply.

"Then who are you? Where did you come from?" Lucius asked. "Show me your ship."

"We didn't come on a ship," Beth said.

"You see?" Tarek said. "They are from merchant families."

"Could be," Lucius said as he rubbed his beardless chin. He looked at Patrick and

Beth. "Tell me, where are your parents?"

Beth glanced at Patrick. He looked scared.

"Come now, children," Tarek said. "Tell Prefect Lucius where your parents are."

"They aren't here," Patrick said.

"Tarek smuggled you into our port," Lucius said. "Just as I suspected." Lucius turned to his soldiers. "Arrest them, and put them in the stocks!"

Georgius

Two of the Roman soldiers got off their horses. The men moved toward the cousins.

Patrick's mind raced. He had to quickly think of a plan. But it was no use. They were surrounded.

"Wait, good prefect!" Tarek called out. "They're only children."

"They're yours, then?" Lucius asked. "This is trouble. *Double* the taxes for trying to trick me."

"You don't understand, prefect," Tarek said.

"I think I do," the Roman prefect said.

Lucius walked his horse around a stack of crates. "You could make your trouble go away," he said. "Just give me a crate of your spices."

"Prefect Lucius," Tarek said, "I didn't bring these children to port. It would be unfair to make me pay—"

"Don't speak!" Lucius said. "Soldiers, carry these children to the stocks. And take one crate of Tarek's spices for hiding them."

"What?" Tarek cried. "My village needs all the crates to live! You know this. Please don't, I beg you!"

"Your village will have to live with one less crate," Lucius said with a sneer. "And these children can rot in the stocks for all I care.

Soldiers, take them!"

Patrick moved back from the soldiers. The rope on his shoulder slipped off.

One of the soldiers said, "And he even brought his own rope. We can tie them up with it."

"No, don't!" Beth cried out. "Please."

"Wait!" a soldier on horseback called out.

Everyone stopped and turned.

The soldier urged his horse forward. He quickly got off his mount. The soldier was tall. He had broad shoulders. His arms were large and muscular.

The soldier gave a salute. "Prefect Lucius, may I speak?" the soldier asked.

Lucius frowned. "What is it, Georgius?" he asked.

Georgius said, "We know that Tarek is

an honest man. We also know the needs of
Silene, his village."

Georgius motioned to Patrick and Beth.
"And these two are mere children," he said.
"It would be unjust to put them in stocks.
What of Rome's mercy?"

"You are too soft, Georgius," Lucius said.
"What are these children to you? Castoffs,
throwaways, dogs . . ."

"They need mercy," Georgius said. "Like all
of us."

"More of that *Christos* nonsense!" Lucius
said.

"*Christos*?" Beth whispered to Patrick.

"Does he mean Jesus Christ?" Patrick
whispered back.

A soldier swatted Patrick's head. "Quiet!"
he said.

Lucius said, "I don't care what you believe, Georgius! These children came to port illegally. Tarek must pay the taxes! They must go to the stocks. Later they will be sold as slaves."

"Then *I'll* pay their tax," Georgius said. "And I'll pay for Tarek's spices as well."

⚫ ⚫ ⚫

Lucius and his soldiers, except for Georgius, rode away.

Patrick was surprised by what had happened. He had been sure Lucius would put him and Beth in the stocks.

But this man Georgius had stepped in. "He paid for us," Patrick whispered to Beth.

"I wonder why," Beth said.

Hazi leaned toward them. He said, "Georgius is a strange man. He believes in strange things."

"*Christos*," Sabra said. Her voice was filled with a hint of awe.

Tarek went to the wagon. He climbed onto the front seat. He shook his head and stared at Georgius. "I'll never understand your *Christos*," Tarek said.

Georgius removed his helmet. He wiped a hand over his sweaty brow. "It's simple, Tarek. *Christos* showed me mercy. He paid my debt of sin. So I show mercy by paying the debts of others."

"I have more debts. Would you care to pay for those as well?" Tarek asked.

Georgius laughed. "You have the means to pay your debts. These children don't. Just as we can't pay our debt to God. Only *Christos* can—"

"Yes, yes," Tarek said quickly. "You've told me."

Patrick frowned. "But I don't know how we'll pay you back," he said to Georgius.

"Ah, children," Georgius said, "I don't expect you to pay me back. But perhaps you'll be able to help someone else."

"When?" Beth asked.

"God will show you. At the right time. In the right way," Georgius said.

"All the same, you're foolish to challenge Lucius," Tarek said to Georgius. "He seeks trouble. He hurts those who resist him. You should fear him."

Patrick saw Beth look up at Georgius. Patrick knew she was thinking of Leslie and Rachel. And about what had happened at school in Odyssey.

"Prefect Lucius is the most powerful man in Leptis Magna. And I respect him," Georgius said.

Georgius looked into the sky. Patrick thought Georgius was looking toward God. "But fear him? No," he said. "*Christos* told us not to fear those who can kill our bodies. Instead, we're to fear those who can destroy our souls."

"Those are foolhardy words," Tarek said.

Georgius shook his head. "Before God, I'm bound to challenge evil where it appears," he said. "Our sacred words say, 'My help comes from the Lord, the maker of heaven and earth.' I will keep going . . . or die trying."

"It's a kindness I won't soon forget," Tarek said. "But alas, I must return to Silene. Children, come along!"

Hazi and Sabra climbed into the nearest tarp-covered wagon. They settled into the back.

"What of these others?" Georgius asked Tarek.

Tarek blinked as if he hadn't understood the question. At last he said, "They don't belong to me. You have paid for them."

Georgius said, "They can't stay with me here in Leptis. It isn't safe. Can't you take them? As a favor, since I paid for your spices?"

"More mouths to feed?" Tarek said. "What services can they perform?"

Hazi poked his head out of the wagon. He looked at Patrick. "Can you do sums?" he asked.

"Sums?" Patrick asked.

Beth said, "Math, Patrick. Adding."

"Oh," Patrick said. "Sure."

"See, Father," Hazi said, "he can do your accounts!"

Sabra's head appeared above Hazi's. Patrick thought they looked a little like a totem pole.

"You can cook and sew," Sabra said to Beth. "Right?"

"Is this true?" Tarek asked.

Beth nodded. "I can help in the kitchen. And I can sew a little. But I'm better at vacuuming."

"Vack-you-ming?" Tarek asked.

"Please, Father!" Hazi and Sabra shouted over and over.

Tarek groaned. "I suppose I could take them on," he said.

"Excellent, Tarek!" Georgius said. He clapped his hands loudly.

Sabra and Hazi quickly pulled Patrick inside the wagon. Then they pulled Beth up too.

"Now we can play some more," Hazi said.

"Okay," Patrick said. "But no more hide-and-seek."

Patrick expected the wagon to move, but it didn't.

"Why aren't we going?" he asked.

"It's difficult to move our wagons," Hazi said.

"Wagons?" Beth asked. "Isn't this the only one?"

"No," Sabra said. She lifted the tarp flap and pointed. Dozens of wagons now sat in a line behind them.

The Message

Beth sat in the back of the wagon with Sabra, Hazi, and Patrick. She looked out. The wagons in Tarek's caravan curved like a snake through the sand.

Beth couldn't remember how long they'd been traveling. An hour maybe. She licked her lips. She couldn't get the taste of dust out of her mouth.

"Blech!" Beth said. "Is it always this dusty?"

"Oh no," Sabra said. "It's usually worse. Much worse."

"And when there's a sandstorm," Hazi said, "you can't see or breathe."

"Halt the caravan!" someone called out.

"What is it?" Beth asked. "Are we there?"

"We're still miles from my village," Sabra said. She leaned between the flaps of the wagon covering.

Beth heard hoofbeats. The sound was soft at first. But then it grew louder.

"It's Kadeem, my father's house servant," Sabra said. She ducked her head back inside the wagon. "I fear there's trouble. Come!"

Beth and Patrick followed Sabra and Hazi. The four climbed over piles of cloth to the front of the wagon.

Beth saw a wild-eyed man on a tall brown horse. The horse was shiny with sweat.

"Master Tarek!" Kadeem cried. "You must hurry! The dragon has attacked again!"

Beth turned to Patrick. His mouth hung open.

"It took the young shepherd, Walid," Kadeem said.

"He was tending his flocks. He was taken at sunrise."

"Are you certain it was the dragon?" Tarek asked.

"There can be no doubt," Kadeem said. "There was much blood."

Tarek said something Beth couldn't understand.

"It's worse still," Kadeem said. "The village people are upset. They are demanding more sacrifices!"

"More?" Tarek blurted out. "But we have given over a third of all our sheep."

"Not sheep this time," Kadeem said. "The people fear the dragon is unhappy with our sheep. They believe it wants something else."

Tarek frowned. Beth thought he looked ill.

"Humans?" he asked.

"Not just humans," Kadeem said. "Young ones, like Walid. Children."

Tarek turned suddenly toward Beth and the others. "Tie yourselves down with Patrick's rope. That way you won't fall out. We must hurry!"

● ● ●

Beth finally climbed out of the wagon. Her legs were wobbly as she stood on the ground. She felt as if she was still bouncing in the back of the wagon. The dusty road had just about shaken the wagon to pieces.

"Come!" Hazi called. He raced off after his father.

Beth and Patrick ran into the village behind them.

Pale buildings and columns of stone rose up on either side of them. A great noise came from somewhere ahead. They came upon a large village square. An angry crowd had gathered there.

"That doesn't look good," Beth said.

A fire burned in the center of the square. A tall man stood on a block of stone. He had a long beard, and he was shouting. Beth couldn't tell what he was saying at first.

The crowd parted for Tarek as he rushed into the square. Kadeem, Sabra, and Hazi were right behind him. Beth and Patrick followed after them.

"What is the meaning of this?" Tarek asked. He glared at the man who stood upon the stone.

Beth saw that the man held a knotted rope in his fist. The rope trailed down and looped around the waist of a teenage girl.

"The dragon is from the devil. It has come for Silene!" the man on the stone yelled. "It will take from us again! We must stop it by offering what it wants."

Beth looked from the man back to Tarek. Tarek's face had turned red from anger. He was trembling.

"Aazan!" Tarek cried. "What horror do you speak? Have you forgotten your place?"

Tarek turned and looked at the village people. The villagers lowered their eyes.

Why won't they look at him? Beth wondered.

Tarek turned back toward Aazan. "I'm the patron and protector of Silene!" he said. "Stand down, and let that poor girl go!"

Aazan spat at Tarek's feet. "Protector?" Aazan yelled. "You're gone most of the time!

You don't protect us any longer! Where were you when Walid died?"

"This is madness, Aazan," Tarek said.

"The beast has come upon us once more. But your sheep no longer satisfy it!" Aazan said. "Walid's blood cries out for action!"

"Would you answer death with more death?" Tarek cried. "That's nonsense."

Tarek turned to the crowd. "Take Aazan to the cells!"

Beth looked at the angry crowd pressing in on them. But no one moved to seize Aazan.

"You see, Tarek?" Aazan called out. "You have let us down. They won't heed you. They know the beast will kill us all . . . *unless* we give of our own!"

"Let the girl go!" Tarek yelled. He drew a short, curved sword from a scabbard on his belt. "She is new to the village. You say you want to give the dragon blood. Then why don't you give your own, Aazan?"

Aazan tossed the rope away. The girl scrambled into the crowd. "Yes, perhaps you're right . . ." he said.

"You're thinking clearly now," Tarek said.

Aazan then drew his own sword and said, "It doesn't seek the blood of a newcomer. It seeks the blood of a true child of Silene."

"No!" Tarek shouted.

Aazan's eyes darted around the square. Then he pointed. "Seize Sabra!" he cried out.

This time the crowd moved quickly. Tarek leaped in front of his daughter. But his efforts failed. Three strong men held him off. Tarek's sword fell to the ground.

Hazi leaped upon the weapon. He picked

it up and lunged at one of the men. But the man swung his fist and knocked Hazi aside. The sword fell at Beth's feet. The boy tumbled to the ground, dazed.

Patrick rushed to Hazi.

Beth watched as two red-faced men grabbed Sabra's arms.

They're taking Sabra! Beth thought. *They're going to kill her.* Suddenly Beth remembered Odyssey. In her mind, she was at recess. She watched her friend Rachel cry.

Beth blinked. "No," she whispered to herself. "Not again."

Beth knelt down and picked up the small sword. She looked at the weapon in her hand. She knew she couldn't use it. But what could she do?

My help comes from the Lord, maker

of heaven and earth, Beth remembered Georgius saying. So she prayed a short prayer, *God, please help me and Sabra.*

Beth dropped the sword in the sand.

Sabra screamed and kicked at the men.

Beth hurled herself toward Sabra. But her foot caught a stone. And she tripped. She tumbled headfirst into the stomach of one of the men. He gasped as he fell down.

She rolled and then leaped to her feet. The second man clung to Sabra. Aazan stepped past her to Beth.

"Leave her alone!" Beth cried.

Aazan grabbed Beth's wrist. "You may join her," he said. "Perhaps the beast will enjoy a stranger's blood after all!"

The Daring Ride

"Come!" Hazi whispered to Patrick. "They took my father to the jail. He'll know what to do."

Patrick didn't know how anyone could know what to do. The villagers of Silene had gone crazy. They had taken Beth and Sabra away. Patrick was afraid of what would happen next.

A dragon? he thought. Fear clutched his heart. *Sabra and Beth are going to be sacrificed to a dragon?*

He touched the rope that Whit had given him. *I don't need rope,* he thought. *I need a whole army.*

Hazi led Patrick down a narrow lane. They came to a long white building. It had rows of small round windows. Patrick thought they looked like a spider's eyes.

"Here!" Hazi said. "Help me move these old crates."

Patrick and Hazi gathered crates from the alley. Then they built a stairway of crates up to one of the jail windows.

Hazi climbed up the crate stairway. "Father? Are you there?" he called through a window.

Suddenly a snarling face appeared in the window. "Get away from here, boy!" the angry prisoner said.

Hazi almost fell off the crates. He leaned backward but caught himself at the last second. "Wrong window!" he shouted.

"Look out!" Patrick cried.

Just then, the prisoner reached between the bars. He tried to grab Hazi. This time Hazi fell.

Patrick caught Hazi by the shoulders. But his weight pulled them both to the ground.

Hazi stood and dusted himself off. "Thank you, my friend," Hazi said. "Let's try a different window."

Again and again, Patrick helped Hazi move crates to reach the windows. It took five tries before they found Tarek.

"Father!" Hazi called.

Tarek was at the window in a flash. "Hazi!" he cried. "Thanks be to God! They didn't capture you!"

"Father," Hazi said. "We must do something to save Sabra and Beth. But what?"

"I can do nothing in here," Tarek said. "You must go to Leptis Magna. Find Georgius. He can stop the sacrifice as an officer of Rome. But you must hurry. Go now. Take our swiftest horse from the pasture. Do you know the one?"

"The black one named Coal?" Hazi asked.

"Yes, yes," Tarek said. "Take her and ride!"

● ● ●

The horse ran like lightning. It carried Hazi and Patrick toward Leptis Magna.

Patrick bounced from side to side. Several times he almost fell off. He clung to Hazi in great fear.

They came to a small building just outside Leptis Magna. Hazi climbed down from the horse and went inside. He came back a moment later. He was with a large man.

Hazi explained that the man was his father's friend. The man agreed to stable the horse for them.

"Come," Hazi said.

Patrick slid down from the horse with great pain.

"Are you well?" Hazi asked.

Patrick shook his head. His arms ached and his legs hurt. A few of his teeth felt as if they had come loose.

Hazi patted the horse's side. "She's a wonderful girl," Hazi said. "We made the journey in half the time. Come, we must find Georgius."

The afternoon sun cast long shadows. Patrick and Hazi entered Leptis Magna. They found Georgius outside a large building of pale stone. Barrels were stacked along one side of the building.

Georgius was sharpening his sword on a spinning, round stone.

"Georgius!" Hazi called.

Georgius looked up. "Hazi?" he said.

Hazi bowed. "Georgius, we need your help."

"Please, sir," Patrick said. "They've taken Beth . . . and Sabra!"

"Quick," Georgius said, "tell me what has happened. Did Lucius take the two girls?"

"No, the people of Silene did," Hazi said.

Georgius's eyes narrowed. "Why?" he asked.

Patrick and Hazi told him the whole story.

When they were finished, Georgius sighed.

"Tell me," Georgius said, "have you or your people ever seen this dragon?"

Hazi shook his head. "No," he said. "The creature comes in the night. But several of the shepherds saw a shape in the sky. They said it was a dragon."

"The shepherds could have seen an eagle," Georgius said. "Are you sure it's not a lion?"

"Certain," Hazi said. "Our village has seen its share of mountain lions. But this creature is different. It eats three times more than a lion."

"I suppose it doesn't matter what the creature is," Georgius said. "Your Sabra and Beth are in danger. I will help if I can."

"Can you bring soldiers?" Hazi asked.

"Your entire village may fight us. That

means I'll need at least fifty soldiers. I must ask Lucius to gather that many men."

"Lucius?" Patrick asked. "But won't he throw us in the stocks?"

"*I* will appeal to Lucius," Georgius said. "You'll wait here."

● ● ●

Patrick and Hazi waited for Georgius inside the large stone building. Patrick couldn't tell if they waited ten minutes or an hour. It felt as if it took forever for Georgius to return. But the sun was still shining when he opened the door.

"What did Lucius say?" Hazi asked.

"He refused," Georgius said. He laid a heavy bag on a table. "He won't allow our soldiers to go. He called it 'a silly village matter.'"

"Oh no," Patrick said. "Then what about Beth and Sabra?"

Georgius went on, "But Lucius said that I may leave my post and help. I'm surprised but grateful. God has shown a way."

"You alone?" Hazi asked. He sounded doubtful.

"I'm not alone," Georgius said. "*Christos* goes with me. And I won't go unprotected." He opened the bag and took out heavy pieces of metal. Then he began strapping the metal over his arms and shoulders.

"Will Roman armor be enough against a dragon?" Hazi asked.

Georgius thumped the armor with his hands. "It's a help. But my strongest protection is the full armor of God."

"We'll be with you," Hazi said. "I'm very

good with a dagger."

Patrick said, "And I'm . . ." He stopped to think of what he was good at. He was stuck. He felt the rope on his shoulder. "I can tie some pretty good knots."

"No, lads," Georgius said. "You are both brave. But you can't help with this task. I'll speed ahead."

Georgius looked at Hazi. "Return to your father," he said. "Let him know that I am helping—with God's strength. It may give him hope."

"But we can help," Patrick said.

Georgius put a hand on the boys' shoulders. "Trust that I'll do everything I can," he said. Then he dashed out the door.

Patrick watched the courageous soldier depart on horseback. He felt heaviness in the pit of his stomach.

"We won't be far behind him," Hazi said. He pulled at Patrick's arm.

The two boys stepped into the sunlight. They made their way along the wall of the building.

Hazi suddenly stopped when they came to a corner. He held up a hand.

"What's wrong?" Patrick whispered.

Hazi backed up. "Prefect Lucius is coming!" he whispered.

The Beast

"How can you do this, Aazan?" Sabra cried.
"My father has done only good for the
village!"

Aazan ignored her. He tied Sabra to the
thick wooden post. He gave the ropes a final
tug. Then he said, "You may explain your
father's good deeds to the dragon. Perhaps
the beast will spare you."

Beth was tied to the other side of the post.
She tugged against the ropes, but they held

tight. She looked to her left. The mouth of a large cave looked back at her. To her right was the sea.

"Please let Beth go," Sabra cried. "She isn't from my family. She isn't even from Silene."

"Yet she fought for you," Aazan said. "She attacked one of my men. She has been loyal to you in life. Perhaps she will be loyal to you in death."

A small group of men behind Aazan chuckled.

Beth looked at Aazan and said, "How can you believe that this will satisfy the monster? That's crazy!"

"We shall see," Aazan said and then turned to his men. "We must return to the village before the moon rises."

Sabra cried, "No, you can't leave us to die!"

The men turned their backs on the girls and walked away. Beth watched the glow of their torches. They looked like angry, red eyes. Soon the torchlight could be seen only in the distance. And then, even the torches disappeared into the night.

Beth heard Sabra weeping quietly. Beth wanted to cry too but couldn't. Her eyes went back to the mouth of the cave. "Is that where the dragon lives?" she asked.

"Yes," Sabra said with a sniff.

"How do you know?" Beth asked. She hoped that somehow a mistake had been made. Maybe the dragon lived somewhere else and wouldn't come to eat them.

"One of the villagers found monstrous tracks leading into the cave," Sabra said.

Beth stared at the sandy ground near her

feet. Then she looked around the base of
the post. It wasn't easy to tell what she was
looking at. Not even the bright moonlight
helped much.

She started to look away when
she noticed something. There
were shadowy marks in the dirt.
Tracks, she thought. She squinted
hard.

Each track was bigger than a man's hand.
A whole trail of them led away into a thatch
of scraggly bushes. White fur clung to the
bushes.

Could those be the dragon's footprints?
Beth wondered. But why were they leading
away from the cave and not into it? They
seemed small for a dragon's clawlike feet. At
least what she imagined they would look like.

"Why did you do it?" Sabra asked Beth in a small voice.

"Do what?" Beth asked.

"Why did you try to stop them?" Sabra said. "Why did you stand up for me?"

"It was wrong for the men to take you," Beth said. "I couldn't just stand by and—"

A roar rumbled in the distance. Beth froze.

"The beast!" Sabra cried. She struggled against the ropes.

The roar came again, now louder. Beth felt the vibrations through her entire body.

The two girls turned toward the cave.

The roar came again and then trailed off into a growl.

"Wait," Beth said. "The roar isn't coming from inside the cave. It's from out there. See those bushes?"

The moonlight painted everything a spooky green color. A huge shadow moved slowly behind the branches and leaves.

Beth felt as if ice slivers were sliding down her back. She struggled against the ropes. Sabra also jerked at her ropes. Neither girl could get free.

Beth twisted her body. She hoped to find another way to loosen her bonds. Then something pricked her side. What if the beast was poking her with its claws? She twisted again.

Nothing was there.

Then she remembered. It was the nail file! "Be still, Sabra," Beth said.

"Be still!" Sabra cried. "How can I be still?"

"I have a file," Beth said. "I'll use it to fray the ropes."

"Hurry!" Sabra cried.

Beth pushed against the ropes but couldn't reach the metal file.

Another roar. This time it was loud and fierce. It seemed to silence every other sound in the night.

Beth looked up. The bushes parted. The shadow emerged. It now stood just a few yards away.

The beast had fur as thick as a grizzly bear's. Huge claws stuck out from its four feet. But it had no wings.

It's not a dragon, Beth thought. For a moment, her curiosity overcame her fear. This creature was some kind of gigantic cat. It was like a lion, but it was *much* bigger. Fanglike tusks hung down from its upper jaw.

That's when Beth remembered something

from school about saber-toothed tigers. But this creature didn't have any stripes.

It growled again, and Beth's fear came back. She struggled with the ropes again.

Sabra screamed.

The saber-toothed cat circled around them. It roared. The girls froze.

"Beth," Sabra whispered. "Beth, the file."

Beth squirmed and felt the file move against her hip. It slipped at an angle toward her tied hands. *A little more*, she thought.

The saber-toothed cat growled again in a deep and dangerous tone. Beth craned her neck to see what it was doing. It moved forward. Its nose was just inches away from Sabra's chin. Sabra muffled a scream.

Beth could hear the huge cat sniffing.

Then it padded around to her and did the same thing.

It was close. Beth could see the moonlight reflecting off the cat's huge golden eyes.

Then the cat disappeared from view. *Oh no!* Beth thought. *What's it going to do?*

"My help comes from the Lord," Beth whispered.

"Where is it? What is it doing?" Sabra asked.

Suddenly the saber-toothed cat was in front of Beth again. It roared in her face. The beast opened its mouth wide. Its fangs were as long as her forearm. Beth thought the beast might swallow her whole.

The giant cat backed up and then dropped low to the ground.

Beth had seen her friend's cat do the same thing—right before it pounced.

Beth closed her eyes and braced herself for whatever would happen. She thought of Patrick, her parents, her friends at school . . . and Rachel. But mostly she thought of Jesus. He promised Christians life after death.

Then suddenly, Beth heard a huge roar from somewhere behind her. The roar sounded like a jet engine and thunderclap all in one.

She opened her eyes. The cat's eyes had moved to something beyond Beth. It backed away slowly from Beth and Sabra.

It's scared, Beth thought. *But of what?*

The saber-toothed cat spun around and then darted into the bushes.

"What is that?" Sabra asked, breathless. She looked toward the mouth of the cave.

Beth couldn't speak. There was a loud thump followed by a thud. Beth turned to the cave entrance. It was black.

The sound is coming from in there, Beth thought.

Another loud thud. A crackling sound, too. Rocks broke free from the top of the cave. The rocks fell to the ground in a rain of dust.

Beth stared at the mouth of the cave.

Slowly, two large ovals appeared in the darkness. They were like two yellow embers. Black pupils slashed the middle of each oval. The eyes seemed to hang in a great shadow.

A low rumbling came from the cave. More rocks and dust fell. Next, there was a blast of air.

And Beth saw fire.

The Breakout

Patrick and Hazi hid behind some barrels. Patrick saw Lucius turn the corner. The prefect was with two soldiers.

"You should have seen the look on Georgius's face," Prefect Lucius said. "He couldn't believe I let him go to Silene."

The three men stopped walking. They shared a laugh.

The Romans now stood near Patrick and Hazi.

Patrick was afraid that one would see them.

"Why did you let him go?" one soldier asked. He had thick, dark eyebrows.

"It's simple, Cato," Lucius said. "Georgius believes in fables. First, it's *Christos* . . . Now it's dragons! He can die for them if he wants."

"But Lucius," Cato said, "there really is some giant beast. It's killing animals in Silene."

"Yes. I hope there is," Lucius said. He laughed again.

"You *hope*?" the other soldier asked. "You *want* Georgius to die?"

Patrick leaned forward to see more clearly. The other soldier was tall and sweaty. Thin blond hair stuck out from under his helmet.

"I'm tired of him, Emil," Lucius said. "His religion is hurting the Roman army. The religious men love their God more than they love Rome. Let the dragon have Georgius."

Cato nodded. Then his bushy eyebrows rose. "What if Georgius kills the dragon? He'll save the village and become a hero."

"Then you'll never be rid of him," Emil said. "A dead hero will make Georgius's religion more popular."

Patrick saw Lucius's face turn dark red. "Then we'll put a new plan in place," he said.

"What plan?" Emil asked.

"We'll stop Georgius. We'll march twenty soldiers to Silene," Lucius said.

"Twenty? Why so many?" Cato asked.

"To capture the soldier who left his post," Lucius said. "We'll say he ran off to worship his God."

Emil said, "But you gave him permission—"

Lucius scowled. "Georgius left his post," he said. "He must be punished."

"A very good plan," Cato said.

"Go get the men," Lucius said. "One way or the other, Georgius will die tonight."

● ● ●

Hazi grabbed the horse's reins. He leaned close to its ear. "Hurry, Coal!" he whispered. "We must warn Georgius!"

Patrick held on tight. Hazi pushed the horse to reckless speed. The ground was uneven in places. He prayed that he wouldn't fall off.

They came near the village. Hazi shouted over his shoulder, "I think I see Georgius up ahead!"

Georgius's horse was drinking from a bucket. Georgius was holding up one of the horse's back legs. He appeared to be digging at the hoof with a knife.

The boys rode right up to the soldier.

Georgius turned toward them with his knife raised. He seemed ready to fight. But he lowered the blade when he saw the boys.

"What are you doing here?" Georgius asked.

"We overheard Lucius," Patrick said. But he was too breathless to finish.

"He's coming with twenty men," Hazi said. "If the dragon doesn't kill you, they will for deserting your post."

Georgius looked thoughtful for a moment. Then he said, "This changes nothing. The girls must be saved."

Georgius focused on the horse again. A moment later, he freed a sharp stone from its hoof.

"Where are the girls?" he asked Hazi.

Hazi's mouth fell open. "I don't know," he said. "I've never been to the dragon's cave. My father wouldn't tell me where it is. He was afraid I'd be curious and go."

"Your father knows?" Georgius asked.

"Yes," Hazi said.

Georgius climbed onto his horse. "Then take me to him. And hurry!"

● ● ●

The trip back to the cells felt endless. Patrick worried about Beth. They might not reach her in time.

Patrick, Hazi, and Georgius arrived at the jail. Hazi called to his father.

Tarek's face appeared at the cell window. "You've come," he said. "Thank you, Georgius."

"Where are the girls?" Georgius asked. "Tell me how to get there."

"I can only show you," Tarek said. "But I'm locked in."

Patrick suddenly had an idea. He slipped the rope off of his shoulder.

"Catch my rope," Patrick said to Tarek. "And tie it to the bars in the window." He tossed the coiled rope toward Tarek. The man caught it and pulled it into the cell.

Georgius said, "Good idea, Patrick. The horses can pull the bars out with your rope."

Patrick blushed with pride. But then he frowned. *I should have thought of this sooner,* he thought. *It would have saved time.*

Soon Tarek had the rope tied to the

window bars. He tossed both ends of the rope back to Patrick.

"Tie each rope end to a saddle," Georgius said. "We'll pull out the bars. But first let me loosen the mortar."

Georgius stood on a crate so he could reach the window. He pulled a dagger out of his belt. He used the dagger's blade to loosen the mortar around the window. Chunks of mortar fell to the ground with soft thuds.

While Georgius worked, Patrick and Hazi tied the rope ends to the saddles.

Patrick was afraid that someone would hear the scraping.

"What's going on?" someone called from inside. "What's that sound?"

"Hurry!" Tarek said. "A guard is coming!"

"Hazi, get on your horse!" Georgius cried.

Hazi climbed onto Coal.

Patrick moved away from the horses.

Georgius jumped off the crate. He raced to his horse. Then the soldier leaped into his saddle. "Now!" he shouted.

Both Hazi and Georgius spurred their horses. The horses suddenly moved away from the wall. The jerk tore the window bars out of the cell wall. And there was Tarek.

Hazi's father climbed through the hole. He used the crate as a step and jumped to the ground. He climbed in front of Hazi onto Coal.

The merchant took the reins and dashed away.

Georgius grabbed Patrick's arm. The soldier swung him onto his horse. They left the village of Silene in a cloud of dust.

Dragon's Fire

A burst of flame shot out of the cave and hit the bushes. The bushes exploded.

The saber-toothed cat leaped from its hiding place. It gave a great roar and a cry. Fire licked its back and its hind legs.

The giant cat rolled on the ground for a moment. Then it struggled to its feet. A growl rumbled in its throat.

The saber-toothed cat arched its back and stared at the cave. It roared at the darkness.

There was a shuffling sound inside the cave. The saber-toothed cat backed up.

Beth tensed as the massive shadow lumbered out of the cave.

Sabra cried, "The file, Beth!"

Beth fumbled around to reach the file in her pocket.

Suddenly the moon slipped out from behind a cloud. The light poured onto the creature. It was coming out of the cave.

Beth couldn't take her eyes off it.

Greens, purples, blues, golds, and silvers—all of these colors reflected off the beast's skin.

Beth blinked. She couldn't believe her eyes. *It truly is a dragon*, she thought.

It was twice the size of an elephant. But it was leaner and more muscular. Its tail and neck were long and thick. They swayed like huge tree branches.

The dragon's head was long and diamond-shaped. Sharp teeth filled its narrow jaws. Its head looked like a cross between a horse's head and an alligator's.

Smoke trailed upward from its nostrils. Beth thought she saw sparks when its teeth rubbed together.

The dragon's attention was on the saber-toothed cat. The dragon roared, and Beth felt the ground shake.

The saber-toothed cat snarled and backed up. It hissed once and scratched at the air with its massive paw.

Beth sucked in a gasp of air. The dragon was coming forward. It walked past the girls. Beth's hand was shaking. But she finally got her fingers around the file. *Thank you, Mr. Whittaker,* she thought.

Beth grasped the file firmly. Then she started sawing the ropes.

The saber-toothed cat may have been frightened, but it didn't give in. It sprang at the dragon's neck.

The dragon swung its head like a hammer. The blow knocked the saber-toothed cat into the air. It hit the ground with a hard thud. Then it rolled to its feet.

The dragon snorted and shook its head. Then Beth saw three bloody streaks across the dragon's snout. The saber-tooth had scored a hit.

The giant cat crouched for another strike.

Beth sawed at the ropes again. One strand was now thin. She yanked with all her might, and the strand lengthened. Suddenly, one of her hands slipped free. Then the other. She leaned over to cut at the rope around her legs.

The dragon opened its mouth wide and let out a loud cough. Once, twice . . . and then a burst of flames shot forward.

The saber-toothed cat screeched and scrambled out of the way. It ran as far as the water, and then it turned back.

Beth untied the last of the ropes from around her legs. She was finally free. She turned to Sabra and untied her friend's ropes. Sabra was free in less than a minute.

The two girls ran for the only cover they could find: inside the cave. They squeezed behind a large rock.

"Is this a good idea?" Beth asked.

"We must think of a way to escape," Sabra said. "And we can't let those horrible creatures see us."

They peeked out at the dragon and the saber-toothed cat. The cat was prowling back and forth in front of the dragon. It seemed to be looking for an opening to strike.

"Do you think the saber-tooth attacked the sheep . . . and your shepherd?" Beth asked.

Sabra nodded. "The claw marks around the post were too small to belong to the dragon."

"And the tracks," Beth said. "Those were paw prints. And the white fur in the bushes. The dragon was being blamed for the saber-tooth's work."

The dragon's roar shook Beth and Sabra

out of their conversation. The two creatures were watching each other.

"What do we do?" Beth asked.

"I see no way out," Sabra said.

The saber-tooth leaped for a strike. The dragon countered with another blast of fire. Red and orange flames lit up the girls' faces.

A strange whining sound came from behind them.

"Did you hear that?" Sabra asked. "It's coming from deep in the cave."

"Uh-huh," Beth said and then swallowed hard. She looked back into the cave.

Shimmering light seemed to be coming from deep in the darkness.

"I see moonlight. I think there's a back way out," Beth said. She didn't like the idea of going deeper into the cave. But it was their only way to get away from the beasts. She slowly moved into the darkness. Sabra came up behind her.

They rounded a wide bend in the cave wall. Then they came to a huge chamber. Small fires were scattered around the room. The firelight reflected on the surface of a wide pool of water. Beth could smell seawater. "I think there's a way out," she said. "But we'll have to swim across."

"No," Sabra said. "There could be an undertow. We could be dragged out to sea."

Then Beth gasped

and pointed. At the edge of the water was a small dragon. It lifted its head sleepily.

"A baby?" Sabra said.

The small dragon turned toward her voice. It blinked at the girls and whined again.

"The dragon was protecting its baby from the saber-tooth," Beth said.

A bright flash from behind them made the two girls jump.

Heavy thumps echoed throughout the cave and shook the floor.

"The dragon!" Beth cried.

They flattened themselves against the cave wall. Beth found a crack in the wall to slide into. She pulled Sabra after her.

The mother dragon thundered into the

chamber.

The baby dragon screeched. Its mother moved toward it and made a deep trilling sound.

Beth thought it sounded almost like a purr. The beasts pressed close to nuzzle each other.

"Time for us to go," Beth whispered.

Sabra nodded.

The girls edged toward the cave opening. They'd made it only a short distance when the dragon roared.

Dust and small rocks fell from the ceiling.

Beth turned in time to see the mother dragon rushing toward them. It was snorting hot flames.

"Run!" Beth screamed.

Battle at the Cave

The moonlight was still bright overhead. Patrick sat behind Georgius on a gray, spotted horse. Georgius carefully guided his horse across the uneven ground.

Tarek and Hazi kept pace on the black mare, Coal.

"The place of sacrifice is just ahead," Tarek called out.

They raced over the hill. And then the horses were reined to a stop. The four friends were near the wooden post. Georgius leaped from his horse and drew his sword. It glinted in the pale moonlight.

"There are tracks here!" he shouted. The Roman soldier knelt by the post and searched the ground.

Tarek and Hazi climbed off Coal. She suddenly reared up, whinnied, and then bolted away.

Tarek gave a shout. "The horse!"

Georgius's horse suddenly jerked its head. It bucked Patrick off and galloped after the mare. Patrick hit the ground hard.

Patrick groaned. Horses always seemed to run away when trouble was near. At least they did in the movies.

"Should we chase them?" Tarek called.

"No," Georgius replied. He looked up. His

eyes were dark and serious. "There is fresh blood here."

Patrick stood up. His chest tightened with worry. "Where are the girls?" he asked.

"My poor daughter," Tarek cried. He bent low to the ground.

Hazi went to his father and put a hand on his shoulder.

A roar sounded from the mouth of the nearby cave. It sounded like a cannon blast.

Patrick stumbled backward. Hazi and Tarek moved toward him. Georgius stepped forward. He stabbed his spear into the ground. Then he lifted the shield from his back. He gave the shield to Tarek.

"Protect yourself," Georgius said. He grabbed his sword. Then he faced the cave.

Slanted, golden orbs of light appeared in

the darkness.

"Stay clear!" Georgius shouted.

Patrick, Tarek, and Hazi huddled together.

Tarek moved in front of the boys to protect them. He gently pushed them backward. Soon they were pressed against a large rock. Tarek held up the shield. The three watched, staring at the cave.

The dragon crept out of the darkness. Its scales glimmered many colors in the moonlight. It reared back on its tree-trunk hind legs and spread its wings wide.

The dragon seemed to triple in size. The wings looked strange to Patrick. They reminded Patrick of bat wings.

The dragon roared again. It snorted and sprayed flames high into the air.

Georgius stood in battle position. His

sword and spear were held ready.

The dragon charged forward. It swiped at Georgius. The soldier knocked away its sharp claws with his spear.

But the dragon's blow broke the spear. It also knocked Georgius off his feet. The soldier rolled to the ground. Then he leaped back to his feet again.

The dragon came at Georgius again with a roar. Georgius raised his sword and faked to one side. Then he jabbed at the dragon's neck.

The beast dodged. But the blade sliced its cheek. Gleaming green and silver scales fell to the dirt.

The dragon spun violently. Its mighty tail whipped around. It slammed into Georgius. The soldier was thrown like a rag doll.

Georgius slammed against a rock wall. He collapsed on the ground.

The dragon turned toward the others.

Tarek held up the shield to cover the boys. "Be brave," he said. His voice quavered.

The dragon moved forward. Its head lifted.

Then a shout came from behind the beast.

Georgius raised his sword. "You will not have victory over me!" he cried out. "I am a servant of God Most High! By His hand I will defeat you!"

The dragon swung around. It responded with a short burst of flame. Georgius moved toward the dragon, avoiding the fire.

Then Patrick heard shouts.

Two small shapes came out of the cave and moved into the moonlight.

"Beth . . . Sabra!" Patrick called out.

The Dragon's Fate

The dragon turned its head toward the girls and roared. For the moment, it seemed to forget about Georgius.

That's when the soldier acted. He rolled beneath the creature's wing.

Beth gasped. Georgius would easily thrust the blade into the dragon's belly. It would be a fatal stroke.

"No, wait!" Beth cried out.

"Don't kill it!" Sabra shouted.

Georgius looked at the girls. He seemed confused. The dragon now seemed to notice that Georgius was beneath it. It began to move.

Georgius twisted his sword to strike.

"Please, Georgius!" Beth shouted. "The dragon is a mother! She's protecting her baby!"

Georgius hesitated again. The dragon leaped aside. Georgius lost his moment to attack. He scrambled to his feet.

The dragon backed away as if it had been cornered. The girls were on one side. Georgius stood in front. Tarek and the boys were on the other side. "Kill the beast before it kills again!" Tarek shouted.

Georgius raised his sword.

"It isn't the killer, Father," Sabra shouted.

"There's a great cat!"

"It's a saber-toothed cat!" Beth yelled.
"Bigger than a lion with teeth like swords!"

Georgius hesitated again.

The dragon seemed to be watching the
exchange between the humans. It was as if
it didn't know which way to strike.

Georgius lowered the sword a few inches.

Beth cried out, "Georgius, she just wants
to defend her home! Please, don't kill her!"

"Move away from the cave!" Georgius
shouted to the girls.

Beth moved first. She made her way along
the rock wall toward Patrick and Hazi.

The dragon suddenly swept back its wing
and came at Georgius.

"Look out!" Patrick shouted.

The blow from the dragon knocked

Georgius backward,
toward the sea. The
soldier's sword went
flying.

The dragon roared
and let out a burst of
flame. Tarek rushed
forward. He shouted
wildly. He waved
the shield and his
arms around like a
madman.

The dragon turned
its attention to Tarek.
That gave Georgius
time to scramble

for his sword. As he did, he shouted at Sabra, "Circle around to the boys. Get away from the cave!"

Georgius grabbed his sword again. He thrust his sword at the dragon. The dragon turned toward the Roman soldier.

Sabra reached the other children.

"There's a crevice in the rock wall," Beth said. "We can hide and watch from there."

The four children positioned themselves in the crack. They watched Georgius and Tarek. The men distracted the dragon, first one way and then the other.

Georgius waved his sword

wildly.

Tarek shook the shield and shouted again.
The dragon backed away from them.

"They won't kill her, will they?" Sabra asked.

Patrick said, "I think they're trying to
drive it back into the cave."

"Look!" Hazi shouted.

The dragon was centered in the mouth of
the cave.

Georgius shouted "Now!" and he charged
with his sword. Tarek also lunged forward
with the shield held high.

The dragon moved backward. She
stumbled farther into the opening of the
cave. Her head struck the cave's ceiling.
There came a terrible rumbling sound.

"Run!" Georgius shouted to Tarek. The two
men scattered.

The roof of the cave began to crumble. Huge rocks came rolling down.

The dragon screeched. It withdrew farther into the darkness. More rocks fell. The ceiling of the cave collapsed. Dust dulled the moonlight.

The dragon and the cave vanished.

Lucius's Lies

Beth and Patrick stood in front of a pile of stones. The entrance to the cave was gone.

Beth watched as Sabra and Hazi embraced their father. Sabra lightly touched his blackened clothes and wept.

Tarek hugged his daughter. Then he said, "Hopefully that will be the last of the dragon."

Beth wondered if the cave really did have a way for the dragons to escape. There was the pool of water. Could the dragons swim out to sea? She had thought she saw moonlight in the back of the cave. She hoped there was really another opening.

Georgius sheathed his sword. Then he stepped up to the children. "Tell me about the great cat," he said.

Sabra and Beth took turns explaining about the saber-toothed cat. Beth finished by saying, "The dragon came out and fought off the cat. The dragon saved our lives."

"Where is this great cat now?" Tarek asked. He seemed nervous as he looked around.

The girls looked at each other. "We don't know," Sabra said. "But its prints are here."

The five of them kept watch

for the great cat. They dusted themselves off and checked for wounds.

"I thought for sure you'd been eaten," Patrick whispered to Beth. He pulled a leaf out of her hair. "I'm glad you're okay."

Beth smiled. "It was scary," she said. "But I really don't think the dragon would have done us any harm."

Georgius held up his shield. It was scorched and bent. "I may have this mounted on a wall. To remember what happened here and give God the glory."

Somewhere in the darkness, they heard a noise. It sounded like hooves thudding in the dirt. A moment later, two horses wandered into view.

"Cowards!" Tarek said to the horses.

Georgius's gray horse wandered over to

the soldier. It nudged Georgius with its nose as if to apologize. Georgius patted its head. "I forgive you."

"We should return quickly to Silene," Tarek said. "For safety. And to rejoice over our victory."

Georgius helped Beth and Patrick up onto one horse. Tarek helped his children onto the other. The two men took the reins and walked in front of the animals. They moved away from the cave and the post. Everyone was glad to leave the scene of the terrible battle.

"There's the traitor!" a voice suddenly cried out. It came from the crest of a hill.

"Oh no!" Patrick cried.

"What's going on?" Beth asked.

"It's Lucius," Patrick said. "He's here to kill

Georgius."

Soldiers on horseback thundered toward them. A few held flaming torches. They circled the weary group.

"Stop where you are!" Lucius commanded. He steered his horse toward Georgius.

"What is the meaning of this?" Tarek asked.

"Georgius, you are under arrest for treason!" Lucius said. He stayed on his horse and faced Georgius.

"Treason?" Georgius asked calmly. "On what grounds?"

"You left your post," Lucius said. "You probably came to plan more smuggling with the merchant."

"You know why I came here," Georgius said. "You gave me permission to leave."

"Lies!" Lucius snapped. "I forbade you to go. Emil and Cato will agree with me."

Two soldiers rode forward.

One said, "Georgius turned his back on Rome and left the army."

"Just so," the other said. "Georgius is a traitor."

"That's not true!" Patrick called out.

Everyone turned toward Patrick.

"I overheard the prefect's plan to get rid of Georgius!" Patrick said and pointed at Lucius.

"Mind your place, boy!" Lucius said. "I can still put you in the stocks."

"I heard it too!" Hazi said. "I was there. I saw Prefect Lucius . . . and those other two." He pointed to Cato and Emil.

Patrick said, "Lucius said he hoped the

dragon would kill Georgius. And if it didn't, he would have Georgius killed for treason."

"More lies!" Lucius cried out.

"Patrick speaks the truth," Hazi said. "We were behind the barrels. We heard these three men make their plans."

A low wave of whispers and muttering went through the soldiers.

"It's Roman law for Georgius to be given a trial," Tarek said. "We will testify on his behalf. He's a noble and honorable man. We'll speak the truth on his behalf."

"Silence!" Lucius shouted. "I am prefect! I command you to arrest Georgius!"

No one moved. The soldiers hesitated and looked at one another.

"Emil! Cato! Arrest him!" Lucius said.

Emil and Cato nudged their horses

forward. They looked unsure.

"If there is a trial," one said, "we would also have to testify."

"There are harsh penalties for giving a false witness," the other said.

The two soldiers looked at Lucius.

Even in the torchlight, Beth could see Lucius's face turn bright red. "There will be no trial if he's dead!" he shouted. He raised his sword, spurred his horse, and charged at Georgius.

Beth watched helplessly. Georgius didn't have time to pull his sword from its sheath.

The Saber-tooth

"No!" Patrick shouted.

Georgius sidestepped Lucius's attack.

Lucius and his horse rode past Georgius.
He stopped on the slope next to the
collapsed cave.

Georgius followed.

Lucius circled his horse around. The two
men were now at a distance from the others.
They faced each other in the pale moonlight.
Patrick watched them nervously.

"You won't draw your sword to protect yourself?" Lucius asked.

"I will not," Georgius said. "My God will be my Protector."

"Foolish man," Lucius said. He lifted his sword again. Suddenly, his horse snorted and reared up. It backed up as if in a panic.

"Stop, you stupid animal!" Lucius cried out. He struggled to hold on to the reins.

"It senses something," Patrick said to Beth.

So did Georgius. He drew his sword and looked around.

"Ha! You will fight me!" Lucius said.

"Watch out!" Georgius shouted.

There was a sudden growl. Then a shadow leaped from the cliff above Lucius.

Patrick couldn't see clearly. One moment Prefect Lucius was about to charge at

Georgius again. The next moment his saddle was empty. His riderless horse galloped past Georgius.

Beth screamed, "The saber-tooth!"

Patrick saw a huge barrel-shaped creature. It was all fur, muscle, and teeth. The beast raked its claws across Lucius's shoulder. It tore the armor free.

Lucius screamed in pain. The soldiers' horses began to buck. The soldiers held on to the reins to keep from being thrown off. Georgius's horse moved back and forth unsteadily. Patrick took the reins and pulled them tight.

There was another growl, and Lucius screamed again.

Georgius threw himself forward. He thrust his sword in front of him. He reached down

and grabbed Lucius's sword with his other hand.

The creature turned toward Georgius and pounced. Georgius leaned aside and thrust both swords upward. One of the blades slashed along the cat's side. The saber-tooth yowled as it rolled and then sprung to its feet.

Georgius took an attack position and lifted the two swords.

The saber-tooth charged again. Georgius thrust the swords at the animal. He reached too far and almost lost his balance. The saber-tooth slashed its claws across Georgius's upper arm.

Georgius cried out. One of the swords was knocked away.

"Somebody do something!" Patrick shouted.

But the soldiers were having trouble controlling their horses. Even Tarek fought with his black mare. He tried desperately to keep it from throwing Hazi and Sabra.

The saber-tooth came at Georgius again. Georgius stepped back. His foot caught on a root, and he fell. The beast roared and pounced.

Patrick watched wide-eyed. Beth screamed.

The great cat landed on top of Georgius.

Beth pressed her face into Patrick's back. "I can't watch," she cried.

Patrick didn't know what to do. He couldn't bear to see Georgius hurt. And yet he couldn't look away.

The saber-cat's weight and muscle seemed to crush the soldier. But the cat didn't move. Everything was still for a moment.

The beast shifted suddenly. Then it fell to one side and lay still on the ground. Georgius's sword was buried deep in its chest.

Georgius slowly stood and looked over the dead creature.

Patrick dared to smile.

Cheers erupted from the soldiers.

Georgius staggered over to Lucius and knelt beside him. The prefect hadn't moved during the fight. Georgius pressed his hand against Lucius's chest.

"Hurry! His heart is still beating," Georgius called out. "He's alive!"

● ● ●

Lucius was taken to Tarek's house in Silene.

Tarek and Georgius tended his wounds.

Lucius's shoulder and arm had been clawed by the saber-tooth. But Georgius announced that the prefect would live.

The next day, the soldiers placed Lucius on a stretcher. They carried him to a wagon for the return to Leptis Magna. The prefect seemed to be in pain. But he was awake.

Patrick and Beth came close to the wagon. They hadn't come to say good-bye. They hoped only to hear what Lucius might say.

"Well, Lucius?" Tarek asked. "What will you do with Georgius? He saved your life!"

"A life for a life," Lucius said. He gestured for Georgius to step forward.

Georgius came alongside the stricken man.

"You risked your life to save me. And I was going to put you to death," Lucius said in a harsh whisper. "I don't understand it."

Georgius leaned forward. "It's the way of *Christos*," he said.

Lucius closed his eyes. "Yes, well, you give me something to think about," he said. "The charges against you are dropped."

"May God bring you back to good health," Georgius said as he stepped back.

A soldier snapped the reins, and the wagon lurched forward. The soldiers on horseback followed the wagon. All of them saluted Georgius as they passed.

Good-byes

"Everyone looks so happy," Beth said.

The four children and Tarek were in front of Tarek's home in the village. They sat on cushioned benches beneath a canopy.

Everywhere she looked, people were dancing, singing, or clapping. Every shop in the village was open. Marvelous foods and drinks were freely shared on every corner. The carcass of the saber-tooth hung on poles in the square.

"Silene hasn't been this happy in all my life," Sabra said. She snuggled up next to her father.

"What happened to Aazan?" Beth asked.

"He was arrested. Aazan will sit in prison for a long time," Hazi said.

"Yes," Tarek said. "But we must be certain that Silene never again turns on itself. Georgius said he will establish a Roman outpost here. It will help to keep the peace."

"Where is Georgius?" Patrick asked.

"We'd like to talk to him again before we leave," Beth said.

"You're going so soon?" Sabra asked.

Beth nodded. She expected the Imagination Station to appear at any moment.

"For that, I'm sad," Tarek said.

"We all are," Sabra said.

"Georgius has gone to the cells," Hazi said. "He's showing our builders how to construct more sturdy prison cells."

Patrick and Hazi laughed. Beth wasn't certain why.

"Well, then, my friends," Tarek said, "we must give you something to remember us by. And to express our thanks for all your brave help."

"No, you don't have to do that," Beth said.

"Don't be silly," Sabra said. "It's our custom."

"What will we give them, Father?" Hazi asked.

"I would offer you the saber-tooth carcass. But it has already begun to stink," Tarek said. He reached into one pocket of his robe . . . then another . . . and another.

Beth wondered just how many pockets the man had.

"Ah, here they are!" Tarek said.

Tarek held out his hand to Patrick and Beth. In his palm were what looked like two oval pieces of metal. One gleamed blue in the rising sun's light. The other shone green.

"What are they?" Patrick asked.

Beth recognized them. "Scales from the dragon," she said.

Tarek said, "You may recall that Georgius struck the creature a hard blow. These scales broke free. They're yours now."

"Whoa!" Patrick said. He admired the blue scale. "This is amazing."

Beth stared down at the purple scale in her hand. She thought about all that had happened. She'd trusted God and tried to defend Sabra. That decision almost cost her life. But God had taken care of her. He even used a dragon to save her!

⊙ ⊙ ⊙

Beth and Patrick found Georgius at the cells just as Tarek had said. The Roman soldier had a trowel in his hand. He was smoothing some kind of plaster on a new cell wall.

Patrick said, "You're fixing the wall we broke?"

"Of course," Georgius said. He placed the trowel in a bucket. "I broke it. Now it's my responsibility to fix it."

Patrick picked up a trowel. "I guess we'll get to repay you after all," he said.

He and Beth helped finish the wall repairs.

The three of them worked silently. Soon the wall was fixed.

After they were done, Beth said to Georgius, "Thank you for everything."

"I'm honored to have been found worthy to help you," Georgius said. "God often takes me on adventures. But I never thought I'd face a dragon and a saber-tooth. And all in one night!"

"You've taught us a lot," Beth said.

Georgius bowed slightly. "No more than you've taught me," he said. "I've never met such brave children."

Beth heard a low hum. The Imagination Station was nearby.

Patrick nudged her gently. "We have to go," he said.

"Do you want me to escort you to wherever

you must go?" Georgius asked.

"No, thank you," Beth said. "We'll be safe now."

"In that case, go with the Lord," Georgius said. "He is Maker of heaven and earth."

● ● ●

Beth and Patrick went to the Imagination Station. The cousins took their places inside. Beth was just about to close the door. But something outside caught Beth's eye.

Patrick had seen the same thing. "Look!" he said and pointed at the sky.

The sun had risen close to midday height. But the sky was a deep blue. In the distance flew two creatures.

Too large to be birds, Beth thought.

"The dragons," she whispered.

Patrick pulled on a lever. The door closed the dragons out of view.

He pushed the red button. And everything went black.

14

Whit's End

Whit was sanding a piece of wood at his workbench. He turned around as the cousins stepped out of the machine.

Their clothes had returned to normal. Both wore jeans and cotton T-shirts.

"Welcome back!" Whit said. "How was your adventure?"

The cousins took turns telling him everything that had happened.

He listened with his hands shoved into

his pockets. When they finished, he drew out his hands and opened them to Patrick and Beth. A shiny scale sat in each palm.

Patrick looked closely. "Is that what I think it is?" he asked. "We saw some of those in Silene . . ."

Whit nodded and handed the scales to Patrick and Beth.

They thanked him.

"So you got close enough to see a dragon's scales?" Whit asked.

"We got close, all right," Patrick said. "A little too close."

"But you stood up to it," Whit said.

Beth knew Whit was thinking of Rachel. And what had happened earlier with Leslie Wazzek.

"Yes," she said. "And I learned that

dragons don't always have scales. Sometimes they're Roman prefects. And sometimes they're village bullies. And sometimes they have fur and really long fangs."

Whit chuckled. "That's true," he said. "The point is to stand up for what's right, no matter what."

"But we don't have to stand alone," Beth said. "Georgius helped me remember that God is my help when I face trouble."

"Then the adventure was worth taking?" Whit asked.

Patrick nodded.

"It sure was," Beth said.

Patrick held up his dragon scale. "Maybe I'll put this on a chain," he said. "It'll remind me to be brave."

Beth looked down at the dragon scale in her hand.

"That's a good idea," she said. "I'll do that too."

"I've got one more thing," Whit said. He went to a shelf and pulled off a book. "I think you'll find this story familiar." He handed the book to Beth.

Beth took the thick blue book. She showed it to Patrick. The title was *The*

Many Legends of Sir George and the Dragon.

Patrick blurted, "Was Georgius really Sir George?"

Whit tapped the cover. "The legend has many forms. In some of them, George is a knight. In others, he's a Roman soldier."

"Does the dragon die in any of the stories?" Beth asked.

"Some of the time," Whit said. "But often Sir George tames the dragon and brings it to the village."

"I like our version," Beth said. "I don't think a real dragon could be tamed."

Whit raised his white eyebrows. "What about humans who act like dragons?" he asked.

Patrick answered, "I think Lucius finally learned to listen to Georgius."

Beth looked at the floor and shuffled her feet. It was hard to admit that she should try to be friends with Leslie Wazzek.

"Beth?" Whit asked.

She said slowly, "I think I'll give my dragon scale to Leslie as a gift. Maybe it's time I told her about *Christos*."

Whit smiled at her.

Patrick said, "About these new dragon scales . . . The ones we got on our adventure disappeared in the Imagination Station. Where did you get these two?"

"From a dragon," Whit said. "Where else?"

Beth asked, "But how . . . ?"

Whit had a merry twinkle in his eyes. "Let's go upstairs for some ice cream, shall we?"

Questions about Dragons

Q: Are dragons mentioned in the Bible?

A: In Revelation 12, the Bible describes a red dragon with seven heads. The creature will appear during the last days of the world.

Q: Could dragons have been a kind of dinosaur?

A: Some people believe that dragon legends arose from ancient sightings of flying dinosaurs, called *pterosaurs*. But no dinosaurs breathed fire.

Q: Was Georgius (Sir George) a real person?

A: History books are full of stories about brave knights and soldiers. However, Sir George was probably not a real person.

For more info on dragons and Georgius, visit *TheImaginationStation.com*.

Secret Word Puzzle

Beth and Patrick found a dragon in this story. Now you can go on your own hunt. Find the Hunt for the Devil's Dragon words in the letter grid on the next page. (The words are hidden top-to-bottom or left-to-right.) Cross out the letters of those words. The leftover letters will show you where to find: "My help comes from the LORD, the Maker of heaven and earth."

   Write the leftover letters, in order, on the spaces below. The answer is the secret word (Don't key in any numbers.)

__ __ __ __ __ 121:2

1 cave
2 Christos
3 cell
4 dragon
5 file
6 horse
7 prefect
8 rope
9 saber
10 soldier
11 wagon

```
P P W S C A D C
R S A C A F R H
E A G E V I A R
F B O L E L G I
E E N L L E O S
C R R O P E N T
T M H O R S E O
S O L D I E R S
```

AUTHOR WAYNE THOMAS BATSON divides his time between family, teaching, and writing. He also likes to read, golf, play video games, travel to the beach, play electric guitar, and create 3D artwork.

AUTHOR MARIANNE HERING is the former editor of *Focus on the Family Clubhouse*® magazine. She has written more than a dozen children's books. She likes to read out loud in bed to her fluffy gray-and-white cat, Koshka.

ILLUSTRATOR DAVID HOHN draws and paints books, posters, and projects of all kinds. He works from his studio in Portland, Oregon.

Interview with Rachel Batson, an author's daughter

Q: What's it like when your dad is writing?

A: He makes me get him soda, refill his ice water, or get him snacks.

Q: What creative contributions did you give to *Hunt for the Devil's Dragon?*

A: In the first draft, my dad had the kids playing Slaves-and-Masters. I told my dad I thought they should play Hide-and-Seek instead. Well, he left in Slaves-and-Masters, and the editor changed the game to Hide-and-Seek. See? I was right.

For more of this interview, go the **TheImaginationStation.com.**

Welcome to the Holy Land in the first century. Patrick meets a young prince from Persia on a secret mission. Beth winds up in a palace, serving a king who is a little bit crazy and over-the-top angry. All the while, events unfold that reveal the Baby Jesus is in danger—and the cousins are the only people on earth who know it. Can Patrick and Beth warn Mary and Joseph in time to keep the newborn King safe?